Pupsicles!

Nancy, Bess, and George walked until they came to a big snowy field. It was empty except for something tall and white.

"Maybe it's a snowman," Nancy said. "Let's check it out."

"Hey!" George said. "That's not a snow-man. It's a snow *dog*!"

"He looks so real!" Nancy gasped.

"Wait a minute," Bess said slowly. "Doesn't this dog look just like Mr. Grubby Paws?"

Nancy walked around the dog to get a closer look. "It does," she agreed. "Same long ears. Same sweetheart tag—"

"Then it's true! It's true!" Bess cried. "Rebecca turned that poor dog into ice. She *is* a snow queen!"

The Nancy Drew Notebooks

THE
NANCY DREW
NOTEBOOKS®

#46

The Snow Queen's Surprise

CAROLYN KEENE
ILLUSTRATED BY JAN NAIMO JONES

Published by Aladdin Paperbacks
New York London Toronto Sydney Singapore

This book is a work of fiction. Any references to historical events, real people, or real locales are used fictitiously. Other names, characters, places, and incidents are the product of the author's imagination, and any resemblance to actual events or locales or persons, living or dead, is entirely coincidental.

First Aladdin Paperbacks edition February 2002

Copyright © 2002 by Simon & Schuster, Inc.

ALADDIN PAPERBACKS
An imprint of Simon & Schuster
Children's Publishing Division
1230 Avenue of the Americas
New York, NY 10020

The text of this book was set in Excelsior.

Printed in the United States of America
10 9 8 7 6 5 4 3 2 1

ISBN 0-7434-3666-0

The Snow Queen's Surprise

1

First Day, Worst Day

Winter is my favorite season!" eight-year-old Nancy Drew shouted. She clapped her mittens together. A mist of snow tickled her nose.

"Mine, too," Bess Marvin said. "Besides summer, spring, and fall!"

George Fayne tossed a handful of snow into the air. "And we have a whole week to have fun in all this snow," she said. "Are we lucky or what?"

Nancy knew they were. It was Monday and the first day of winter break. It was also the day after a really big snowfall.

The three friends had come to the park.

It was filled with kids pulling their sleds and racing down hills.

"Let's bring our sleds to the park tomorrow," Nancy suggested.

"Cool!" Bess said. "But what should we do today?"

"We can make snow angels," George suggested. She adjusted her red hat over her dark curls.

Bess shook her head. "But that means lying in the snow. And getting snow all over my new purple parka," she complained.

Bess smoothed the pockets of her parka. She was wearing a matching hat over her blond hair.

George rolled her eyes. "What are parkas for, Bess?" she joked. "The beach?"

Nancy giggled. Sometimes she couldn't believe that Bess and George were cousins. Bess had a closet full of pretty clothes. George's closet was filled with jeans and soccer balls.

"Would you rather build a snowman, Bess?" Nancy asked.

"No," Bess said. Her blue eyes sparkled. "I want to build a snow *queen*."

George wrinkled her nose. "What does a snow queen look like?" she asked.

Bess pointed over Nancy's shoulder and gasped. "Like that!" she said.

Nancy spun around.

Walking toward them was a girl wearing a white coat with a fluffy white collar. On one of her hands was a furry white muff. In the other was a wand with a sparkly snowflake on the tip. A shimmering tiara crowned her head.

"That's no snow queen," George said as the girl got closer. "That's Rebecca."

The girls knew Rebecca Ramirez from school. She was also in the third grade at Carl Sandburg Elementary School, but in a different class. Rebecca wanted to be an actress.

"I am *so* a snow queen!" Rebecca declared. "I'm playing one at the Twinkling Stars Drama School."

Nancy knew about Rebecca's drama school. It was on Main Street. The kids met twice a week after school, on Saturday, and even during winter break.

"Why are you wearing your costume in

the park, Rebecca?" Nancy wanted to know. "Is the snow queen play today?"

"No," Rebecca said. "We start rehearsals on Wednesday. But it's never too early to practice my part."

Nancy watched as Rebecca waved her wand and twirled around.

"What do snow queens do?" Bess asked. "Besides making people dizzy."

Rebecca stopped twirling. "For one thing," she said, "snow queens can turn anything into ice."

"Great!" George joked. "Then make us snow cones. Cherry, lemon, and lime."

"In winter?" Bess giggled. *"Brrr!"*

Rebecca put her hands on her hips. "It's true," she said. "We can turn anything into ice. And anybody!"

"As in . . . people?" Bess asked.

Rebecca nodded. "People and—"

"Woof!" a bark interrupted Rebecca.

Nancy pushed her hat up from her forehead. She saw a big dog peeking from behind a tree. His tail wagged as he leaped over the snow toward the girls.

"Where did *he* come from?" Bess asked.

Nancy thought the dog was beautiful. His fur was the color of butterscotch pudding. His long ears looked very soft.

"Look." George pointed. "He's wearing a heart-shaped tag. That means he belongs to someone."

Nancy knew not to pet strange dogs, but she gave him a big smile. "Hi, boy!" she said. "You sure look friendly."

The dog looked at Nancy with warm brown eyes. Then he turned and hopped over the snow toward Rebecca.

"What does he want?" Rebecca asked.

The dog jumped. His paws landed on Rebecca's shoulders. He barked playfully at her snowflake wand.

"I think he wants to be a snow queen," Bess said with a giggle.

"Down!" Rebecca shouted.

The dog's ears flattened against his head. He whined and backed down.

"You scared him," Bess scolded.

Nancy saw two brown smudges near Rebecca's shoulders. Rebecca saw them, too.

"Oh, no!" Rebecca cried. "That dumb dog

got dirty paw prints all over my snow queen costume!"

"Yuck," Bess said. "I'm glad he didn't jump on my new purple parka."

The dog seemed puzzled. He tilted his head and looked at Rebecca.

"He didn't mean it, Rebecca," Nancy said. "He was just being a dog."

"A *bad* dog," Rebecca added. She raised her wand over the dog's head.

"What are you doing?" George asked.

"What does it look like I'm doing?" Rebecca asked. "I'm casting a snow queen spell over Mr. Grubby Paws."

Nancy sighed. Rebecca was taking her part of snow queen a little too seriously.

"Sugar is sweet, snow is nice," Rebecca began to chant. "Turn this pesty dog into ice!"

Rebecca pointed the wand at the dog. He turned and ran behind a row of bushes.

"That will teach all dogs not to jump on me," Rebecca declared. "And if they do—Pupsicles!"

"Pupsicles?" Bess repeated.

Rebecca tried rubbing out the stains with her hand.

"Don't worry, Rebecca," Nancy said. "Those stains will come out."

"And if they don't," George said with a shrug, "cast a spell on them."

"Very funny," Rebecca grumbled. Then she turned to leave.

"Where are you going?" Nancy asked.

"To meet my mom at the Double Dip," Rebecca replied. "Even snow queens need a hot chocolate break once in a while."

Nancy's mouth watered. The Double Dip made the best ice cream in River Heights, and the best hot chocolate in winter.

The three friends watched Rebecca walk away in the snow.

"Nancy? George?" Bess asked slowly. "What if Rebecca's spell worked?"

"Worked?" Nancy asked. "Rebecca was just play-acting—the way she always does."

"Sure," George agreed. "Remember when Rebecca played a cow in the first-grade play? She wore a bell around her neck for a whole week."

"But what about the dog?" Bess asked. "Mr. Grubby Paws?"

Nancy thought the name was funny. She

decided to call him Grubby.

"Grubby probably ran back to his owner," Nancy said. "But we can find him if it will make you feel better."

"It would," Bess said.

First the girls checked behind the bushes. Grubby was nowhere in sight.

Next they walked deeper into the park. There were more kids pulling sleds and building snowmen, but no Grubby.

"Come out, come out, wherever you are!" Nancy called.

The girls walked until they came to a big snowy field. It was empty except for something tall and white.

"Maybe it's a snow-covered water fountain," George guessed.

"Or a snowman," Nancy said. "Let's check it out."

But as they got closer . . .

"Hey!" George said. "That's not a snowman. It's a snow *dog!*"

Nancy could see that George was right. The hard snow was shaped to look like a long-eared dog with a collar.

"He looks so real!" Nancy gasped.

"Wait a minute," Bess said slowly. "Doesn't this dog look just like Mr. Grubby Paws?"

Nancy walked around the dog to get a closer look. "It does," she agreed. "Same long ears. Same sweetheart tag—"

"Then it's true! It's true!" Bess cried. "Rebecca turned that poor dog into ice. She *is* a snow queen!"

2

Snow Queen or No Queen

No way!" Nancy said, shaking her head. "Rebecca did not turn Grubby into ice. And she is *not* a snow queen!"

"Not until she changes all three of us into snow cones," Bess said. "Cherry, lemon, and lime."

Nancy smiled at Bess. She was usually scared pretty easily, but George wasn't.

"There has to be a reason for this snow dog," Nancy said. "Right, George?"

George didn't answer. Her dark eyes were still glued to the snow dog.

"Huh?" George said.

"I said, there has to be a reason for this

dog," Nancy repeated. "Right?"

"Don't know," George said. "But in the meantime, I'm staying away from Rebecca Ramirez."

"Me, too," Bess said.

"But Rebecca is our friend," Nancy argued. "She lives near me."

Bess and George didn't seem to listen. They spoke in serious tones.

"We should tell a grown-up what Rebecca did," Bess said. "But not her parents. They might have the same powers."

"I know!" George said. "Let's tell Rebecca's acting coach, Stella Logan. She ought to know that her snow queen is a real one."

Nancy couldn't stand it anymore. "Time out," she said. "Rebecca does not have special powers, and I'll prove it."

"Prove it?" Bess asked slowly. "You mean like solving a mystery?"

The word "mystery" made Nancy smile. She loved solving mysteries more than anything. She even had a blue detective notebook where she wrote all of her clues.

"Yes," Nancy said. "Proving that Rebecca

isn't a snow queen will be like solving a mystery."

"But how are you going to prove it, Nancy?" George asked.

"Hmm." Nancy tapped her chin thoughtfully. Then her eyes lit up. "I'll start by following Rebecca around and watching her real close."

Nancy reached into her pocket and pulled out her detective notebook. She carried it everywhere she went.

"Then," Nancy went on, "I'll write all of the reasons why Rebecca *can't* be a snow queen. Any questions?"

"Just one," Bess said. "Does this mean we're not going sledding tomorrow?"

"Bess!" George sighed.

The girls walked to a nearby bench. They brushed off the snow and sat down.

Nancy opened her notebook. A pencil with a kitten eraser was tucked inside.

She turned to a fresh page and wrote "Rebecca is *not* a snow queen" on the top.

"What if you get clues that Rebecca *is* a snow queen?" George asked.

Nancy didn't think she would, but a good detective was prepared for anything.

"I'll make two lists," Nancy said. "Then we'll see which one fills up first."

Nancy wrote "Rebecca *is* a snow queen" on the opposite page.

"You'll have to work fast, Nancy," George said. "If Rebecca *is* a snow queen, she can turn River Heights into a giant snow globe by tomorrow."

"And shake it, too!" Bess added.

"Okay, okay," Nancy said. "Today is Monday. I'll prove that Rebecca isn't a snow queen by . . . Wednesday morning."

"And if you don't?" Bess asked.

"I will!" Nancy said with confidence. "But if I don't, then we'll write a letter to Stella Logan. All about Rebecca."

"*Then* we'll go sledding," Bess said.

Nancy smiled as she shut her notebook. The girls walked back to the snow dog to look for more clues.

Nancy studied the dog from the top of his head to the tips of his paws. That was when she noticed something unusual.

"Look!" Nancy cried. "There's something

carved into the dog's paw!"

Nancy, Bess, and George almost bumped heads as they bent down to look.

The design was carved to look like a leaf—a leaf with a curled stem.

"Maybe Grubby had a leaf on his paw before he turned into snow," Bess guessed.

"Maybe not," Nancy said. "But however that leaf got there, it's a clue."

Nancy wasn't sure which list to add the leaf to. So she carefully drew the leaf on a clean page.

"Don't forget to write the snow dog clue in your notebook," Bess said. "On the 'Rebecca *is* a snow queen' page."

Nancy didn't want to add a clue to that page, but she had to be fair.

"Okay," Nancy said. She wrote the clue in her notebook. She held it up for Bess and George to see.

Then suddenly—

TWACK!

Nancy gasped. Something had knocked her detective notebook right out of her hand!

3

Frost Fright

Hey!" Nancy cried as her notebook landed in the snow with a thunk.

"That was a snowball!" George said through her teeth. "And I think I know who threw it."

Nancy thought so, too. She turned and saw Jason Hutchings, Mike Minelli, and David Berger. They were standing behind a big mound of snow. The snow was so high it came up to their shoulders.

"Surrender now!" Jason shouted. He waved another snowball over his head.

"Or risk another attack by the Chill

Commando!" David called.

"The boys!" Nancy groaned.

Most of the boys in Nancy's class were nice. But Jason, David, and Mike were always making trouble.

The boys snickered as they held up handfuls of wet snowballs. They were all wearing wool caps. Jason's was red, Mike's was green, and David's was blue.

"Should we fight back?" Nancy whispered to her friends. "We beat them in a snowball fight once before."

"We don't stand a chance," Bess said. "This time they have a fort."

"And I have an awesome pitching arm," George said, scooping up snow.

George grunted as she pitched a snowball. The girls laughed as it knocked Jason's red cap right off his head.

"This means war," Jason muttered.

Nancy helped George scoop up more snowballs. But Bess stood on the side.

"Come on, Bess," George ordered. "Put some hustle in your muscle!"

"You know I hate snowball fights," Bess

complained. "And I'll get snow all over my brand-new purple parka."

"Here we go again!" George groaned.

Nancy didn't feel like throwing snowballs either. Not when she had a new mystery to work on. So while George threw the snowballs she talked about her plan.

"Let's get some hot chocolate instead," Nancy said as they ducked another flying snowball. "My dad gave me some money before I left this morning."

"Great," Bess said. She looked around. "Hilda's hot chocolate van is probably parked here somewhere."

The girls always bought hot chocolate from Hilda. But this time Nancy had another idea.

"Let's go to the Double Dip," Nancy said. "Then we can drink hot chocolate *and* question Rebecca."

"Good idea," George said loud enough for the boys to hear. "And we won't be anywhere near the *Chimp* Commando!"

"That's *Chill* Commando!" Jason called, hurling another snowball.

"Not when you're always monkeying around!" Nancy called back.

The boys laughed. They scratched their heads and made monkey noises.

"I wish Rebecca would turn Jason, David, and Mike into ice," Bess said as they walked out of the park.

"I told you—Rebecca is not a snow queen," Nancy said. "Just a drama queen."

The Double Dip was a few blocks from the park. Main Street had been shoveled. But the girls still had to stomp snow off their boots before going inside.

"There she is!" Bess whispered when they were inside. "There's Rebecca!"

Nancy saw Rebecca sitting at a table and drinking hot chocolate. Mrs. Ramirez was talking to a woman at another table.

"Hi, Rebecca!" Nancy called.

Rebecca waved back. She was still wearing her white snow queen coat.

"Hi," Rebecca said. She pointed to her shoulders. "Look! I got rid of that yucky dog stain."

"And the *dog*," George whispered.

"*Shh!*" Nancy warned.

The girls stepped up to the counter. They ordered three hot chocolates with extra marshmallows. Very carefully they carried their cups to Rebecca's table.

"It's cold outside," Rebecca said.

"Yeah," George said. "My toes feel like pupsicles—I mean—Popsicles!"

Nancy saw Rebecca's snowflake wand lying on the table. She decided to get right to the point. "What else do snow queens do, Rebecca?" she asked. "Besides turning things into ice?"

Rebecca licked off a hot-chocolate mustache. "Instead of tears," she said, "we cry icicles."

George whistled. "That's got to hurt," she said.

"And we have shimmering sleighs," Rebecca said. She waved her hand. "Sleighs that fly high through the winter sky!"

Nancy didn't believe it. But Bess and George were staring at Rebecca with wide eyes and open mouths.

"Why aren't you drinking your hot chocolate?" Rebecca finally asked.

"Too hot," George blurted.

"Yeah," Bess said. "I blew on it, but it's still too hot."

"That's because you're not a snow queen," Rebecca said with a smile. "Snow queens breathe clouds of ice crystals."

"What?" Bess gasped.

Rebecca took a deep breath. She leaned over the table and blew on all three hot chocolates. She blew so hard that a marshmallow popped out of George's cup.

"Hey!" George complained as the marshmallow landed in her lap. "I was going to eat that!"

"Sip it now," Rebecca said.

Nancy picked up her cup. She was about to sip when she heard loud snorting noises. Looking up she saw Jason, David, and Mike by the counter. They had sodas in their hands—and straws up their noses!

"Oh, gross!" Bess cried. "Now they're pretending to be walruses."

"They probably followed us here," George grumbled, "so they could bother us some more."

Bess turned to Rebecca.

"Can't you turn the *boys* into ice,

Rebecca?" she asked. "Pretty pleeease?"

"Bess!" Nancy complained.

But Nancy's warning came too late. Rebecca grabbed her snowflake wand. She waved it as she spoke in a low, deep voice . . .

"From the tops of their heads to the tips of their toes," Rebecca chanted. "Turn David, Jason, and Mike into snow!"

Not again, Nancy thought.

"Rebecca," Mrs. Ramirez called. "It's getting late. We'd better fly."

"Fly?" Bess squeaked.

"Coming, Mom," Rebecca called back. She smiled at Nancy, Bess, and George. "I have to go now. Bye."

The girls watched as Rebecca and her mother left the Double Dip.

"Did you hear that?" Bess whispered. "They're going to *fly!* Probably in their flying sleighs."

"This I've got to see," George said.

Nancy, Bess, and George jumped up and scrambled for the door. They pressed their noses against the glass and looked out.

Nancy could see Rebecca and her mom climbing into a beige minivan.

"There!" Nancy said as the van drove off. "Rebecca and her mom did not fly."

Bess and George looked a bit disappointed.

The girls walked back to their table. Jason, David, and Mike were two tables away, noisily slurping their sodas.

"And the boys weren't turned into snow either," Nancy pointed out.

"If only!" Bess groaned.

George took a sip of her hot chocolate. Her dark eyes popped wide open over the rim of the cup.

"Is it still too hot?" Nancy asked.

"No," George gulped.

She put down her cup and stared at Nancy and Bess. "It's too cold. *Ice* cold!"

4

A Bark in the Park

C old?" Nancy repeated. How could that be? They had left their cups for just a minute or two.

Bess quickly took a sip. "My hot chocolate is icy cold, too!" she cried.

"Try yours, Nancy," George said.

Nancy picked up her cup. Then she slowly took a sip.

"Well?" Bess asked.

Nancy didn't want to admit it. But . . .

"It's cold," she said.

"Maybe Rebecca was telling the truth," George said, her voice shaking. "Maybe she *does* have icicle breath!"

Nancy stared at her cup. The cold hot chocolate was weird. But she refused to believe that Rebecca had cast a spell.

"It had to be Rebecca," Bess shivered. "Who else could have done it?"

Nancy thought of the boys.

They were good at hurling spitballs and snowballs. And doing gross things in the school lunchroom. But how could they turn hot chocolate cold? How could anyone?

"I don't know how it happened," Nancy admitted. "It's a mystery."

"Then you have to write this clue in your notebook," Bess instructed her. "On your 'Rebecca *is* a snow queen' page."

Nancy sighed. A clue was a clue, whether she liked the clue or not.

She pulled out her blue detective notebook. On the line under the snow dog she wrote the words "Cold hot chocolates."

Now there were two clues that Rebecca was a snow queen. But Nancy refused to give up.

"Let's meet in the park tomorrow morning," Nancy said. "At ten o'clock."

"To go sledding?" Bess asked with a little jump.

"No," Nancy said. "To look for Mr. Grubby Paws. The *real* Mr. Grubby Paws!"

"Daddy, do you believe in magic?" Nancy asked later that evening.

Nancy and Mr. Drew were eating dinner at the kitchen table. They had just finished bowls of Hannah's special vegetable barley soup.

Hannah Gruen had been the Drews' housekeeper for five years. She had taken care of Nancy since Nancy's mother had died.

"Magic?" Mr. Drew asked. He had a twinkle in his eyes. "You mean like this?"

Mr. Drew showed Nancy his empty palm. Then with the same hand, he reached out and pulled a quarter out of Nancy's ear.

"Abracadabra!" Mr. Drew said.

Hannah put her hands on her hips. "How did you do that?" she asked.

Nancy was surprised, too. Her father was a lawyer, not a magician.

"It's magic," Mr. Drew said. He gave the quarter to Nancy and smiled.

"Thanks, Daddy!" Nancy said.

But deep inside Nancy was worried.

If her father could perform magic, then why not Rebecca Ramirez?

After dinner Nancy played a video game with her dad. Then before going to sleep, she found a story about a snow queen in her big book of fairy tales.

Rebecca was right, Nancy thought as she read in bed. Snow queens do ride in flying sleighs—and turn people into ice.

"But it's a fairy tale!" Nancy insisted out loud. She shut the book and went to sleep.

The next morning Nancy, Bess, and George met in the park. The snow was just as high as it was the day before.

"Here, boy!" Nancy called. She cupped her mittens around her mouth. Then she called for the dog again.

"Here, Grubby!" Bess called.

"That's not how you call a dog," George said. "Watch this!"

Nancy and Bess covered their ears as George let out a shrieking whistle.

"George!" Bess complained. "This isn't a soccer game—"

"Woof!" a dog barked.

"Grubby?" Nancy gasped. She spun around excitedly—until she saw a tiny brown poodle running over.

"False alarm," George muttered as the dog ran back to its owner.

"Let's go to where we saw Grubby yesterday," Nancy suggested. "Maybe that's where he likes to play."

The girls' boots made deep footprints in the snow as they walked. When they were halfway through the park, George stopped.

"Check it out," George whispered. "The boys' fort is still there."

Nancy frowned when she saw the hill of snow. Sticking up from behind it were three wool hats—red, green, and blue.

"Oh, great," Nancy whispered. "They're getting ready to strike again."

"Not unless we beat them to it," George whispered. "Let's sneak around the fort with our own snowballs."

"A surprise attack!" Bess squealed. "Goody gumdrops!"

"I thought you didn't like snowball fights, Bess," Nancy said.

"I don't," Bess said. "But I don't like Jason, David, and Mike even more."

With handfuls of snowballs, the girls walked quietly around the fort. Nancy wondered why the boys were so quiet.

But when Nancy looked behind the fort she saw why. Instead of the boys there were three snowmen!

"I don't get it," George said. "They're wearing the boys' hats."

"And they have straws up their noses," Nancy said slowly.

"Hey," Bess gulped. "Are you thinking what I'm thinking?"

"I am," George said, nodding. "Rebecca did it again. She cast a spell on Jason, David, and Mike—and it worked!"

5
Chill Out!

No way!" Nancy said, shaking her head. "The boys were at the Double Dip when Rebecca cast that spell."

"Some spells may take longer to work," George said. "The boys could have gotten to the park and—*poof!*—pests on ice!"

"It's all my fault!" Bess cried. "I told Rebecca to freeze Jason, David, and Mike. And she did it."

"But anyone could have built these snowmen," Nancy said. "The boys could have built them themselves."

"And leave their hats in the park?" George asked.

"Maybe," Nancy said. "Why don't we go to their houses and look for them?"

"No!" George said.

"Why not?" Nancy asked.

"Because what if it's a trick?" George asked. She narrowed her eyes. "What if they're waiting in Jason's front yard—with snowballs?"

"Oooh, no!" Bess said.

"Then we'll go to my house and call them," Nancy said.

George nodded. "Let's do it."

"Wait," Bess said. "Nancy has to write this clue in her notebook."

Nancy's heart sank. Another clue on the "Rebecca *is* a snow queen" page!

But instead of writing, Nancy doodled three tiny snowmen in her notebook. It made them all giggle.

As they walked out of the park they passed the snow dog. It was still frozen.

"*Brrr.* I don't know if I'm shivering from the cold," Bess said, "or because I'm so scared."

"I know," Nancy said. "Let's tell some jokes. Then we won't be so scared."

"I know a good one," George said with a grin. "What did the policeman shout as he chased the Popsicle bandit?"

"What?" Nancy asked.

"Freeze!" George said.

"Freeze?" Bess wailed. "George Fayne— that's not funny!"

"Sorry." George sighed.

When the girls reached Nancy's house, Hannah greeted them at the door.

"Don't take off your boots yet, girls," Hannah said. "One of your friends is waiting for you in the backyard."

"Who?" Nancy said. "Katie Zaleski? Molly Angelo?"

"It's Rebecca Ramirez," Hannah said. "Last I looked she was playing with Chip."

Nancy gulped. "Rebecca . . . is with Chip?" she asked.

"Uh-oh," Bess groaned.

The girls raced around the house to the backyard. Rebecca was standing under a tree. She was wearing her snow queen coat and carrying her snowflake wand.

"Hi!" Rebecca called as Chip retrieved a twig. "Nancy, your dog is so cool!"

"Cool?" Nancy cried. "As in *cold?*"

Nancy ran to Chip. She pulled off her gloves and began feeling her fur.

"As in neat," Rebecca said, wrinkling her nose. "Is something wrong?"

Nancy shook her head. She straightened up and forced a smile. "Did you come over to play?" she asked Rebecca.

"No," Rebecca said. She twirled her snowflake wand between her fingers. "I'm here to do you all a big, big favor."

"A favor?" Nancy, Bess, and George repeated at the same time.

"I've decided to make every day a snow day," Rebecca said. "That means no school and lots of snow to play in for a whole year."

"But I *like* summer!" Bess pouted.

"You'll get over it," Rebecca said. She raised her wand in the air. "Now, get ready, because I'm about to perform the dance of the never-ending snowflakes."

The girls stepped back as Rebecca began to twirl around and around. When she stopped she tapped each elbow with her wand. Then she tapped each foot.

Chip barked as Rebecca used her wand to form a big circle in the air.

"North winds gust, north winds blow," Rebecca called. "I command to make it snow! And snow! And snow! And snow!"

Rebecca fell dramatically on the clean snow. She closed her eyes and didn't move.

"It's not snowing," Bess whispered.

Chip began to lick Rebecca's face.

"Yuck!" Rebecca cried. She jumped up and dusted herself off. "I'd better go."

"Why?" Nancy asked. She wanted to watch Rebecca as much as she could.

"I have to read my snow queen script," Rebecca said. "Tomorrow is the first day of rehearsals."

Rebecca gave a little wave. Then she walked around the house.

"Nancy?" Bess said. "You got scared when Rebecca was with Chip, didn't you?"

"Sort of," Nancy admitted.

When it came to Chip, she wanted to protect her from everything: cars, candy, even possible snow queens!

"Does that mean you're starting to believe Rebecca, too?" George asked.

"I'm not sure what I believe anymore." Nancy sighed. "All I know is this . . ."

"What?" Bess asked.

"It's still not snowing," Nancy said.

The girls looked up at the sky. It was gray but no flakes were in sight.

"Girls!" Hannah called out the window. "Come in for some tomato soup!"

"Yummy!" Bess cried.

The girls entered the Drews' house through the back door. They took off their boots and hung up their jackets. Then they all washed their hands and sat down in the warm kitchen.

"There's nothing like hot soup on a cold day like this," Hannah said as she poured thick red soup into three bowls.

"Thanks, Hannah!" Nancy said.

She opened the box of salty crackers on the table and handed some to Bess and George. The girls crushed crackers over their soup.

"By the way, Nancy," Hannah said as she washed dishes in the sink. "What was Rebecca doing out there?"

"Some dance," Nancy said, giggling. "To make it snow."

"Well, it seems to have worked," Hannah said. "Look outside."

The giggling stopped. Nancy, Bess, and George stared at one another. Then they jumped up and ran to the window.

"No way!" Nancy gasped as big white flakes fell from the sky.

"It's snowing!" George cried.

"Rebecca did it again!" Bess wailed.

Nancy stared at the snow coming down. How would she ever explain this?

6

Bells and Spells

Hutchings,'" Nancy read aloud. She held the telephone book in her lap as she pushed the numbers. "Four-five-six . . ."

It was late afternoon. Nancy was in the den, calling the boys. She had to prove that they were home and that they weren't snowmen.

Because it was snowing, Bess and George had left right after finishing their soup. But the friends had all planned to meet at the pizza parlor on Main Street at noon the next day.

"Please be home, Jason," Nancy whispered. She waited for the Hutchingses' phone to ring, but it never did. Instead there was total silence.

"That's weird," Nancy told herself. She hung up and found the Minellis' number in the phone book. But when she tried it, the same thing happened. Silence.

"*Too* weird," Nancy said.

She tried the Bergers' phone. It didn't ring either!

Oh, no, Nancy thought. What if Rebecca really did turn the boys into—

Nancy shut the phone book and shook her head. "What was I thinking?" she asked herself. "Rebecca is *not* a snow queen!"

But when Nancy opened her detective notebook she frowned. If Rebecca wasn't a snow queen, why weren't there any clues on her "Rebecca is *not* a snow queen" page?

"Working on a new mystery, Nancy?" Mr. Drew asked as he came into the den.

Nancy took a deep breath. Then she told her father all about Rebecca.

"Rebecca even made it snow, Daddy," Nancy said. "Is that weird or what?"

"Let me show you something," Mr. Drew

said. He picked up a newspaper. "Check out the headline on this morning's paper."

Nancy read the front page out loud: "'More snow today.'"

"The snow was coming long before Rebecca cast that spell," Mr. Drew said.

"Maybe Rebecca saw the headline, too," Nancy said. "And decided to trick us."

Mr. Drew smiled. "Speaking of tricks," he said. "Let me show you how I pulled that quarter out of your ear."

Nancy watched her father tuck a quarter up his sleeve. When he reached out the quarter slipped down into his hand.

"So that's how you did it." Nancy sighed. "You had me worried, Daddy."

Nancy felt better. Not only was she twenty-five cents richer, she had her first clue that Rebecca wasn't a snow queen.

"Fake snow dance," Nancy said aloud as she wrote the words in her notebook.

Mr. Drew looked over Nancy's shoulder. He pointed to Nancy's drawing of the leaf. "What's this?" he asked.

"I found a leaf design carved on the snow

dog's paw," Nancy said. "But I have no idea what it means."

"Hmm," Mr. Drew said. "This leaf could be your most important clue, Nancy."

Nancy got excited. But then she remembered that the next day was Wednesday. Her heart sank. Wednesday meant her time for solving the case would be up!

That night Nancy fell asleep trying to think of more clues. But when she woke up Wednesday morning she had to face the truth—she had not solved the case.

Maybe I'm not such a good detective after all, Nancy thought sadly.

She spent the morning cleaning her room and playing with Chip. When it was close to noon she got permission to meet Bess and George on Main Street.

"You mean you couldn't reach *any* of the boys last night?" George asked in the pizza parlor. "Their phones didn't ring?"

"No," Nancy said. She nibbled her pizza, but she wasn't very hungry.

"Maybe Rebecca turned their whole families into snow," Bess said, tugging a string of cheese from her slice.

"Well, it's Wednesday," George pointed out. "That means it's time to write to Stella Logan."

The girls finished their pizza slices. George pulled some stationery from her jacket pocket. She borrowed Nancy's pen and began to write.

"'Dear Ms. Logan,'" George read out loud. "'There's something about Rebecca Ramirez we think you should know.'"

Nancy didn't want to write the letter. She wanted to write more clues in her notebook and solve the case. But it was too late.

"Done!" George said after she listed all of Rebecca's spells.

The girls decided not to sign their names. George folded the letter and sealed it inside the envelope.

"Let's go straight to the drama school," George said, "and slip this letter under the door."

"Then let's get our sleds and go to the park," Bess said excitedly.

The girls left the pizza parlor. They walked down Main Street until they reached the Twinkling Stars Drama School.

"Who's going to slip it under the door?" Nancy asked.

"Bess will," George said.

"Why me?" Bess cried.

"Because you're the shortest," George said. "And the closest to the ground."

"Whatever." Bess sighed. She took the envelope and began to kneel.

"Yoo-hoo!" a voice piped in.

Nancy and her friends whirled around. Rebecca was walking toward them!

"Some snow last night, huh?" Rebecca said proudly. "What are you doing here?"

"Um," Bess said. She stood up and shoved the letter behind her back.

"We wanted to wish you luck," Nancy said quickly.

"For rehearsals?" Rebecca asked.

Another voice broke in. "Hi, guys!"

This time Nancy saw their friend Katie Zaleski. She was walking out of the pet store. She was holding a cage with her parrot, Lester, inside.

"Lester just picked out a new toy," Katie said. "It is so neat!"

Rebecca leaned over to the cage and

smiled. "Polly wanna cracker?" she cooed.

Lester blinked at Rebecca. Then he opened his beak and squawked, "Ding-a-ling! Ding-a-ling! Ding-a-ling!"

Rebecca's eyes flew open. "Did he just call me a ding-a-ling?" she demanded.

"No, silly," Katie said. "Lester was talking about his new toy bell."

Rebecca glared at Lester and raised her wand in the air. "Birds of a feather flock together!" she shouted. "They turn to ice in frosty weather!"

"Oh, no!" Bess cried. "Not another snow queen spell!"

"He asked for it," Rebecca said with a smile. She opened the door to Twinkling Stars and walked inside.

"What was that all about?" Katie asked, confused.

"Rebecca thinks she's a snow queen," Nancy said. "And that she can turn anything into ice."

Katie rolled her eyes. "That's the silliest thing I ever—"

"*Raaak!*" Lester squawked. He kicked the door to his cage open and flew out.

"Oh, no!" Katie cried as Lester flew down the street. "Lester has escaped!"

The four girls chased Lester as he flew down Main Street. He made a sharp turn into the River Heights Art Gallery.

"Follow him!" Nancy ordered.

Nancy, Bess, George, and Katie ran into the art gallery. A fancy party was being held. There were long tables filled with food and punch. Grown-ups stood near the paintings, talking softly.

Nancy was about to look for Lester when Katie let out a big shriek.

Nancy, Bess, and George ran over to Katie. Her hand trembled as she pointed to a table. On it was a bird made of ice!

"Lester!" Katie wailed. "What has she done to you?"

Nancy stepped back slowly. Had Rebecca really turned Lester into ice?

7

A New Leaf

Lester will never play with his new toy now," Katie wailed. "Never!"

The party guests turned to stare. A man in a black suit hurried over.

"Careful, children," he said. "Don't touch the bird of paradise ice sculpture."

"Sculpture?" Nancy repeated. "You mean someone *made* this?"

"Yes," the man said. His mustache twitched as he grinned. "This bird was made by a very talented artist in River Heights. She sculpts lots of animals."

"Then it's not Lester." Katie sighed with relief.

"Lester?" the man asked. "Who's Lester?"

But Nancy was wondering about the animals. Could the sculptor have made the snow dog in the park, too?

"What's the sculptor's name?" Nancy asked the man.

"Her name?" the man asked. "It's—"

"Arrrk!"

Everyone spun around. Lester was on a nearby table munching from a platter of salmon-spread crackers.

"Lester wanna cracker!" Lester squawked. *"Rraaak!"*

"Lester!" Katie cried happily.

The man in the black suit wasn't so happy. He pointed to the door and in a loud voice said, "Get that bird out of here!"

While Katie swooped up Lester, Nancy glanced at the ice bird. She saw something carved into the bird's wing. It was the same leaf that was on the ice dog.

Nancy felt George tug her arm. Then the friends ran out of the art gallery.

"I'm taking Lester straight home," Katie said, lifting his cage. "He's had enough excitement for one day."

"And enough crackers," George said.

"Ooooh boy!" Lester screeched.

Nancy watched Katie walk away. Then she turned excitedly to Bess and George.

"A leaf was carved on the bird's wing," Nancy said. "The same leaf that was on the snow dog. Isn't that a great clue?"

"Sure, Nancy," George said. "But it's already Wednesday."

Nancy wanted to scream. Why did she promise to solve the case by Wednesday? Why not Thursday? Or even Friday?

"Look," Bess said. She held up a cracker and giggled. "I grabbed this on the way out. Tuna fish salad on an onion cracker."

"Woof!"

Nancy jumped as a big dog bounded over. Without stopping, he snatched the cracker from Bess's hand with his teeth!

"Hey!" Bess shouted as the dog charged away. "That dog took my cracker!"

Nancy stared at the dog. It was butterscotch colored with long, floppy ears—just like Grubby.

"I think that's the dog from the park!" Nancy cried. "Let's follow him!"

The girls chased the dog down Main Street. The sidewalks were slushy and slippery so they had to be careful.

"Stop, cracker thief!" Bess shouted.

The dog made a turn at the next corner. The girls turned the corner, too.

Nancy saw the dog race toward a yellow house with green shutters.

"Woof!" the dog barked as he ran around the side of the house.

"Now he's in the backyard," George groaned. "We can't follow him there."

"I wonder who that dog belongs to," Bess said, out of breath.

Nancy glanced around. In front of the house was a snow-covered mailbox.

"There's one way to find out," Nancy said. She dusted powdery snow off the cream-colored mailbox. On the side a name was painted in green.

"'B. Greenleaf,'" Nancy read out loud. She brushed off more snow. Then her eyes opened wide. Painted next to the name was a leaf. A very familiar leaf!

"There it is!" Nancy said excitedly. She

tapped her hand on the painted leaf. "It's that leaf again!"

"So?" Bess asked.

"So the person who lives in this house might have made the ice bird," Nancy said. "And the snow dog in the park."

"Are you sure the dog we just chased was Mr. Grubby Paws?" Bess asked.

"No," Nancy admitted. She waved her hand in the direction of the house. "But I'm going to find out."

The girls' boots made crunching noises as they walked around the house.

When they reached the backyard they stood perfectly still. The yard was filled with the most beautiful statues made of snow.

"Animals! A castle! Gnomes!" Bess cried. "It's like a fairy tale!"

The girls walked around the snow statues. They were like nothing Nancy had ever seen before.

"And look!" Nancy said. "They all have the leaf design carved into them."

Nancy was about to point to a polar bear

statue when the butterscotch-colored dog jumped out from behind it.

"Oh!" Nancy gasped. The dog nuzzled his nose in Nancy's mitten. He was Grubby all right.

"There you are, Bingo!" a woman's voice boomed.

Nancy saw a woman walking into the backyard. She was wearing a blue parka, gray pants, and dark blue rubber boots. Her green eyes sparkled under her striped wool hat.

"Your dog's name is Bingo?" Nancy asked. It was a lot nicer than Mr. Grubby Paws.

"Yes," the woman answered. "And I'm Betty Greenleaf. Did you come to see my snow sculptures?"

"Sort of," Nancy said. "Did you also make the ice bird at the art gallery?"

"You bet!" Betty said.

Nancy couldn't wait to ask her next question. "And what about the snow dog in the park?" she asked.

Betty nodded. "I made that sculpture of Bingo on Monday morning," she said.

"Yes!" Nancy cheered under her breath. Her father was right. The leaf was the most important clue of all!

"Except Bingo wasn't a very good model," Betty went on. "He kept running off somewhere."

"We know." Bess giggled.

"Now, if you'll excuse me, I have to see if my phone works," Betty said. "Some telephone lines in town were damaged from the snow last night."

Nancy thought back to the boys' phones. No wonder they didn't ring!

The girls thanked Betty Greenleaf. After petting Bingo, they left the yard.

"You see?" Nancy asked. "Rebecca never turned a dog into ice. She is not and never will be a snow queen!"

"High five!" George exclaimed.

The three friends slapped their gloves and mittens together. Then they walked away from Betty's house.

"It's a good thing we never gave Stella Logan that letter," George said.

"That's for sure," Nancy said.

Bess stopped walking. Her face became pale.

"Bess?" Nancy asked. "What's wrong?"

"The letter," Bess gulped. "I slipped it under the Twinkling Stars door."

"You what?" George cried. "When?"

"Right before we ran after Lester!" Bess cried. "We were going to, anyway!"

Nancy hit her own forehead with the back of her hand. "Oh, noooo!" she cried.

8

Rebecca Takes a Bow

I'm sorry!" Bess said. "But we weren't supposed to solve the case today!"

Nancy took a deep breath. "It's okay, Bess," she said. "Let's just get that letter before Ms. Logan reads it!"

The girls walked quickly to Main Street. When they reached the drama school they went inside. The front hall was decorated with posters and pictures of past plays.

Nancy didn't see Rebecca, but she could hear her voice.

"I don't know what you're talking about," Rebecca was saying.

Nancy, Bess, and George followed the

sound of Rebecca's voice to a small auditorium.

"There she is!" George whispered.

Rebecca was standing on the stage. She was surrounded by six kids wearing costumes and headpieces.

"We found this by the door," a boy wearing reindeer antlers said. He waved George's envelope in the air.

"So?" Rebecca asked.

"So what's this about you being a *real* snow queen?" the reindeer boy asked.

"Come clean, Rebecca," a girl dressed as a chicken said. "Did you really turn a dog into snow?"

"And turn hot chocolate cold?" another girl wearing a snowflake garland asked. "No wonder the marshmallows in my cocoa wouldn't melt!"

A tall woman with bright red hair marched in. She clutched a flowered shawl over her black pants and sweater.

Nancy guessed she was Stella Logan.

"Children, children!" she cried. "What is going on here? You know we have to rehearse the dance of the woodchucks."

"Excuse me, Ms. Logan," Nancy blurted. "I can explain everything."

All eyes turned to Nancy.

"You see, Ms. Logan," Nancy began, "Rebecca pretended to have special snow queen powers. And we believed her."

"We even wrote a note telling on her," George said. "We didn't want her to cast any more spells."

"But now we know it's not true," Nancy added. "Rebecca isn't a real snow queen. Just a real girl."

Nancy expected Ms. Logan to be angry. But instead she smiled.

"Bravo, Rebecca! Bravo!" Ms. Logan said, clapping her hands.

"Huh?" Nancy asked.

"Rebecca may not be a snow queen," Ms. Logan explained. "But look how many people believed her. *That* is acting!"

Ms. Logan applauded again. The other students began applauding, too. Rebecca smiled and took a deep bow.

"Wait a minute," George piped up. "Rebecca scared a lot of people with her make-believe spells."

"Even me," Bess said.

Rebecca straightened up. Nancy could see she was blushing.

"Is that true, Rebecca?" Ms. Logan asked. "You know I want all my twinkling stars to shine."

"It's true." Rebecca sighed.

Ms. Logan walked up to Rebecca. She put her arm around her shoulder.

"Rebecca, a good actor knows the difference between real and make-believe," Ms. Logan said. "She saves her magic for the stage."

"Yes, Ms. Logan," Rebecca said. She turned to Nancy, Bess, and George. "I'm sorry I scared you. I guess I got carried away."

"I guess," Nancy said, smiling.

"Who wants to be a real snow queen anyway?" Rebecca said, waving her hand. "I like summer camp too much. And the beach. And lemonade slushies!"

Nancy was glad Rebecca had apologized. Now they could all be friends again.

"One more thing," Ms. Logan said. She turned to Nancy, Bess, and George. "Now that you've met the cast, why don't you come to see our play in two weeks?"

"*The Snow Queen*?" Nancy asked.

"Yes," Ms. Logan said. "I'll give Rebecca three extra tickets just for you."

Nancy, Bess, and George thanked Ms. Logan. They waved goodbye to the cast and left the drama school.

"We did it!" Nancy cried on Main Street. "We proved that Rebecca was not a snow queen!"

"But what about all the other weird things that happened?" George asked.

"Yeah," Bess said. "Like cold hot chocolate. And Jason, David, and Mike—"

"Did someone say our names?" a voice sneered.

Nancy gasped. A shower of wet snowballs fell over her and her friends.

Nancy wiped snow from her eyes and stared at the boys. They were not wearing their wool hats.

"The Chill Commando strikes again!" Jason cheered.

Bess put her hands on her hips. "We thought you were turned into snowmen," she said.

Jason, David, and Mike gave one another high-fives.

"They fell for it!" Jason laughed. "I knew those snow dudes looked like us."

"Especially with those straws up their noses!" David said. He scrunched his nose and gave a walrus snort.

"*You* made those snowmen?" Nancy asked. "The ones behind the fort?"

Jason nodded. "Weren't they way cool?" he asked.

"You also fell for our hot chocolate trick at the Double Dip," Mike said.

"Yeah!" Jason snickered. "When you ran to the door we slipped ice cubes from our sodas into your cups."

Ice cubes! Nancy thought. So that explains it!

"You should have seen your faces." David guffawed. "You were so surprised!"

Nancy saw George scoop up snow.

"You mean like this?" George asked the boys. She reached back her arm and hurled a snowball at Jason.

Nancy and Bess joined in the action. They

threw snowballs as fast as they could make them.

"Hey!" Jason complained.

"No fair!" Mike exclaimed.

"We're not wearing hats!" David cried. He covered his red ears with his hands. "Those things are cold!"

"Surrender, Chill Commando!" Nancy shouted to the boys. "Or risk another attack—by the Snowflake Sisters!"

George threw another snowball. It landed on Mike's head.

"Um," Mike gulped. A chunk of snow fell on his nose. "Let's get some pizza."

"Good idea," David said.

The girls cheered as the boys escaped into the pizza parlor.

"Victory!" George shouted.

"I think I like snowball fights now!" Bess giggled.

Nancy was so happy she wanted to shout. She had solved a case *and* won a snowball fight. All in one day!

"Let's celebrate with some hot chocolate," Nancy suggested. "Some *hot* hot chocolate."

"And then go sledding," Bess said, her blue eyes shining. "Once and for all!"

The girls made their way to the Double Dip. They ordered three hot chocolates with extra marshmallows.

This time while Nancy waited for her cup to cool she took out her notebook. She began to write.

Good news! Not only did I prove that Rebecca isn't a real snow queen, I proved she's a great actress, too.

I also learned that I do believe in magic. No, not the magic of snow queens. The magic of a sculptor right here in River Heights. And she didn't even use a wand—just her own two hands.

Now, *that* is magic!

Case closed.

THIRD-GRADE DETECTIVES

Everyone in the third-grade loves the new teacher, Mr. Merlin.
Mr. Merlin used to be a spy, and he knows all about secret codes and the strange and gross ways the police solve mysteries.

YOU CAN HELP DECODE THE CLUES AND SOLVE THE MYSTERY IN THESE OTHER STORIES ABOUT THE THIRD-GRADE DETECTIVES:

#1 The Clue of the Left-handed Envelope

#2 The Puzzle of the Pretty Pink Handkerchief

#3 The Mystery of the Hairy Tomatoes

#4 The Cobweb Confession

Ready-for-Chapters

COBBLE · STREET

has never
been this much fun!

**Join Lily, Tess, and Rosie on their adventures
from Newbery Medalist Cynthia Rylant:**

The Cobble Street Cousins: In Aunt Lucy's Kitchen
0-689-81708-8
US $3.99/$5.50 CAN

The Cobble Street Cousins: A Little Shopping
0-689-81709-6
US $3.99/$5.50 CAN

The Cobble Street Cousins: Special Gifts
0-689-81715-0
US $3.99/$5.50 CAN

The Cobble Street Cousins: Some Good News
0-689-81712-6
US $3.99/$5.50 CAN

And coming soon from
Simon & Schuster Books for Young Readers:

The Cobble Street Cousins: Summer Party
0-689-83241-9
US $15.00/$23.00 CAN

The Cobble Street Cousins: Aunt Lucy's Wedding
0-689-83242-7
US $15.00/$23.00 CAN

Aladdin Paperbacks • Simon & Schuster Children's Publishing
www.SimonSaysKids.com

HITTY'S TRAVELS

HITTY'S TRAVELS #1: Civil War Days

Hitty's owner, Nell, lives on a plantation in North Carolina. When a house slave named Sarina comes to work for Nell's father, the girls become friends. But when Nell and Sarina break the rules of the plantation, things will never be the same again. . . .

HITTY'S TRAVELS #2: Gold Rush Days

Hitty's owner, Annie, is excited to travel with her father to California in search of gold, but it's a tough journey out West and an even tougher life when they arrive. Annie longs to help out, but is there anything she can do?

HITTY'S TRAVELS #3: Voting Rights Days

Hitty's owner, Emily, lives in Washington, D.C. Emily's aunt Ada and many other women are trying to win the right to vote. But when the women are put in jail, all hope seems lost. Will Emily—and Hitty—find a way to help the cause?

HITTY'S TRAVELS #4: Ellis Island Days

Hitty travels to Italy in style with a spoiled little rich girl, but soon falls into the hands of Fiorella Rossi, a kind girl whose poor family longs to reach America. Will the Rossis survive the awful conditions of their long journey?

Available from Aladdin Paperbacks
Published by Simon & Schuster